Ms. Chievus in the Classroom

written by
Sandip Sodhi

illustrated by
Ken & Janet Priebe

This book is dedicated to my family and friends
who encouraged my mischievous nature.

It is also dedicated to the hundreds of students
who have helped me become the teacher
that I am today.

ISBN 978-1-7770218-0-1

Ms. Chievus
in the Classroom

Ms. Chievus had been warned about Division O-O. No teacher had been able to last even an hour in that class.

"The kids are BONKERS! We don't know what to do anymore." explained Principal Fedup.

Ms. Chievus peeked into the classroom and could not believe her eyes! Ms. Fedup was not joking! What was she going to do?

Paper airplanes zipped by.

Kids were standing on their desks, and others were spitting paper out of the ends of straws!

GROSS!!!

"Do you still want the job?" Ms. Fedup asked.

"Definitely!" exclaimed Ms. Chievus, with a devious smile. "I have a plan!"

Ms. Fedup sighed, "Good luck!" and walked away.

Ms. Chievus took a deep breath, exhaled, took another breath, counted slowly to five, and walked into the classroom.

She walked up to the front of the room, and waited for the kids of Division O-O to give her their full attention. The clock ticked...no one listened!

All of a sudden, she stood up on the desk and screamed "SILENCE!" at the top of her lungs. The students were stunned!

"What just happened? Did she just scream? Is she alright?" they mumbled. Suki turned to Min Joon and yelled, "I think she's strange!"

Ms. Chievus somersaulted off her desk and cracked up laughing.

"You're weird!" called out Ray, the student who moments earlier, was standing on the desk. "You're supposed to be setting an example."

"What's the problem?" asked Ms. Chievus. "Am I not supposed to yell or do gymnastics in the classroom?"

"NOOOO!!!" the students replied.

"Oh, okay." said Ms. Chievus. "I'll write down a list of things that I'm not supposed to do." She started to write down the students' comments on the board...

-don't yell
-don't stand on the desks
-don't do somersaults

Several of the kids' mouths dropped and the lightbulb went off in most of their minds. "We get it! That's what *we* were doing, right?"

Ms. Chievus never said a word. The kids, still stunned, asked Ms. Chievus what they were going to do.

She replied, "NOTHING. No one HAS to do anything. Let's just do NOTHING!"

Huge smiles were planted on the students' faces. The kids thought they had the best teacher ever! No work to do and someone who was even goofier than themselves! The happy energy continued until the bell went.

After the students were dismissed, Ms. Chievus walked down to Ms. Fedup's office and had a little chat.

"Well, that was some day!" Ms. Chievus exclaimed.

"What are you going to do with that class?" inquired Ms. Fedup.

"Well, I have an idea and want to share it with you." said Ms. Chievus slyly.

"I'm ready to hear what you have to say." said Ms. Fedup.

After discussing the ideas for awhile, both adults felt quite optimistic.

"Let's keep our fingers crossed for tomorrow!" said Ms. Chievus.

"Good luck, and let me know if I can help in any way." remarked Ms. Fedup.

The next morning, students were lined up by the door, chatting with great excitement and ready to go to class.

After all the kids were seated inside, Ms. Chievus cartwheeled into the room.

She stood in front of the class and blew huge bubble-gum bubbles as she took attendance.

The pop-popping of the bubbles was quite loud, rude, and annoying, so Raja turned around and shouted, "STOP THAT!"

Ms. Chievus continued blowing bubbles and chewing loudly. Finally, a few of the kids went up to Ms. Chievus and asked her to stop making those sounds.

Ms. Chievus turned and asked Division O-O if it bothered them.

They all yelled, "YES!"

Ms. Chievus turned to the board and added the following to her list:

-I will not make loud sounds.
-I will not chew gum and blow bubbles.

"Also," said Nikkoo, "please don't cartwheel around the classroom – you could hurt someone!"

The class agreed.

Ms. Chievus decided to hop from place to place.

"STOP THAT!" the students exclaimed.

"What's wrong?" Ms. Chievus asked. "I wasn't cartwheeling."

"JUST WALK!" shouted the kids. So, Ms. Chievus added that to the list too.

An hour had passed and the students were getting quite restless.

"Ms. Chievus, what are we going to learn today?"

"Lots of fun stuff!" she exclaimed.

The students started to cheer loudly.

Ms. Fedup was walking by the classroom and heard the commotion coming from the room.

She very sternly asked to speak to Ms. Chievus.

They stepped into the hall and closed the classroom door.

"How's it going in there?" Ms. Fedup asked. "Do you think your plan will work with these students?"

Ms. Chievus enthusiastically replied, "Oh, yes! Hahaha...they are dumb-founded! Now, if you can keep the parents informed, I think we'll have a stellar class in no time at all."

They chuckled, whispered a bit more, and then high-fived one another.

Ms. Chievus walked back somberly into the classroom. The students were concerned. They asked, "Are we in trouble? Is she going to call our parents?"

"No...*I'm* the one who's in trouble. Ms. Fedup said unless I learn to behave and to teach properly, I'll be transferred to another school." Suddenly, she started to sob.

"Noooo! We want you to stay!" yelled the kids. The students were surprised that their teacher was in trouble because of the chaos they had started in the classroom.

The students gathered together and were busy whispering away while Ms. Chievus settled herself down.

"She really cares, and she's a lot of fun." said Sonu. "We have to do something!"

That day, the students vowed to save their teacher.

They had a class meeting and came up with a plan.

A few of the students presented their plan to Ms. Fedup.

After some discussion, Ms. Fedup agreed to consider Division O-O's plan. She said the plan would have to be reviewed every few weeks.

The students were thrilled! They would make sure that Ms. Chievus stayed at the school! Ms. Fedup grinned to herself.

Ms. Chievus had done it!

Division O-O was on its way to being transformed!

ABOUT THE AUTHOR & ILLUSTRATORS

Ms. Chievus in the Classroom is Sandip Sodhi's first book for children. Sandip has been a classroom teacher and teacher-librarian in Surrey, BC for the last 25 years. Sandip loves and encourages laughter wherever she goes. She lives in Surrey, British Columbia with her husband and daughter.

Illustrators Ken and Janet Priebe are a husband-wife team living in Delta, British Columbia with their two children. Janet is a photographer, graphic designer, and watercolour painter who runs her own cake decorating business. Ken is an animator, writer, teacher, illustrator, and author of several poetry books for children.

kenpriebe.com
jaybirdcreations.com

CPSIA information can be obtained
at www.ICGtesting.com
Printed in the USA
BVHW021712021120
592251BV00004B/25